W9-CJS-228

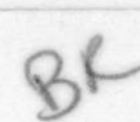

Albert the Running Bear Gets the Jitters

by Barbara Isenberg & Susan Wolf
Illustrated by Diane de Groat

Clarion Books
TICKNOR & FIELDS: A HOUGHTON MIFFLIN COMPANY
New York

Acknowledgment

We wish to thank Antoinette Saunders and Bonnie Remsberg, co-authors of *The Stress-Proof Child*, for their insightful work in the area of stress management for children. In addition we wish to thank both Peggy Roggenbuck Gillespie, author of *Less Stress in 30 Days*, and Margaret Hollander for their respective work in relaxation techniques.

Clarion Books
Ticknor & Fields, a Houghton Mifflin Company

Printed in Italy.

Library of Congress Cataloging-in-Publication Data
Isenberg, Barbara.
Albert the running bear gets the jitters.
Summary: Albert the Running Bear is challenged to a race by a new bully bear at the zoo and has to deal with all sorts of stress symptoms. Includes relaxation techniques.
[1. Bears—Fiction. 2. Stress (Psychology)—Fiction. 3. Bullies—Fiction. 4. Running—Fiction] I. Wolf, Susan. II. De Groat, Diane, ill. III. Title.
PZ7.I774A1 1987 [E] 86-32680
ISBN 0-89919-517-2

NI 10 9 8 7 6 5 4 3 2 1

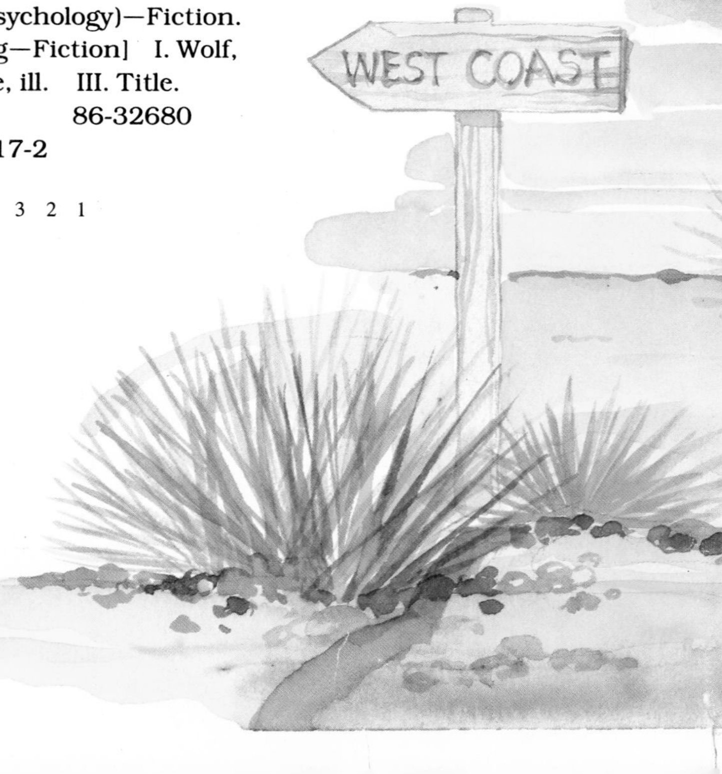

To Odl Bauer for her wonderful spirit and
inspiring talents which, on this occasion,
helped bring Boris to life.
—B.I.

For Michael, Alexandra, Jonathan, Sam and
especially Cecile.
—S.W.

NEWS
ZOO
WINNER
COACH

"I am Albert, the Running Bear, light as a feather, loose as a goose, and faster than a shooting star!" Albert chanted. He bounded across the finish line and raised his arms in victory.

Albert had won every marathon from Monterey to Buzzards Bay.

The crowd carr[illegible]bert to the waiting bus which would take him back to his zoo.

"Congratulations," said Albert's friend, Violet. "You ran your best race ever."

"Thanks to your coaching, Violet."

Success had not spoiled Albert.

"Look who's home!" cried Julia the giraffe as Albert stepped into his cage.

"Hi, Julia!" he called. "Did anything exciting happen while I was away?"

"Let's see," Julia said. "The peanut machine broke down, the price of admission went up and, oh yes, a new bear moved in."

"A new bear?" said Albert. "From where?"

"The wilds of Alaska," Julia reported.

"Oh boy!" Albert said. "I can't wait to meet him."

Albert began to unpack. When he opened his locker, he found a scribbled note taped to the door.

"That's strange," thought Albert as he picked up his new trophy and placed it on the shelf with the others. Another note tied to his bronzed running shoe caught his eye.

"Cream puff!" Albert muttered. As he tore off the note, he bumped into his exercise bike and found a third note speared on the handlebar.

"Who could be writing these?" Albert wondered.

Albert showed the notes to his neighbor.

"I haven't noticed anything suspicious from up here," Julia said.

He showed them to Violet. "It's just a silly prank. The best thing to do is ignore them."

But the taunts kept running through Albert's mind.

"I can't stand it!" said Albert. "I've got to find out who's writing these notes!"

By nighttime, Albert had a plan. He took out a large bag of marshmallows and stuffed them into his jogging suit to look like a body. He tucked the decoy under the bed covers along with his teddy bear. The trap was set!

Albert picked up his flashlight and tiptoed behind his locker to hide. He waited and waited. Just as his eyelids began to droop, he heard heavy footsteps and the sound of a key turning in the lock.

"Got you!" cried Albert, switching on the flashlight. There in the circle of light was the most enormous bear Albert had ever seen. He was holding a note in his paw.

"Who are you?" gasped Albert.

"I'm Boris, the new bear," came the gruff reply.

Boris grabbed Albert's flashlight and swaggered around the cage, touching all of Albert's favorite things.

1
FIRST
PLACE
1st
WINNER

"Where I come from," Boris sniffed, "exercise is for sissies,

teddy bears are for babies,

and marathons are for humans!"

"Well, here at the zoo," Albert said, pulling himself up as tall as he could, "sneaking into someone's cage is called tres-passing,

snitching Keeper Norman's keys is called stealing,

and leaving nasty notes is just plain mean!"

Boris pointed the flashlight at Albert.

"What do you want?" Albert gulped.

"I challenge you to a real race," snarled Boris. "Bear to bear."

Albert took a step forward and clenched his fists to hide his trembling paws.

"I accept," he squeaked. "Just name the time and place, and I'll be there!"

"Meet me on the track Saturday at sunset," Boris growled. "Then we'll see who's the champ around here."

The moment Boris left, Albert collapsed on his bed. He could hear his heart pounding, and he felt short of breath. When he finally dozed off, he had the same nightmare over and over.

In the morning, Albert sat on his bed, biting his claws. "I'd better get hold of myself or I won't be in shape for Saturday!"

He pushed away his untouched breakfast and forced himself out to the track for his daily run. To his dismay, he found all the animals crowded around Boris.

"In the wilderness of Alaska," Boris boomed, "I had to break the ice to catch my dinner like this. . . ."

"To reach the beehives high up in the spruce trees, I had to climb like this. . . ."

"And there were times when I had to outrun hundreds of hunters like this. . . ."

Violet noticed Albert slinking away and followed him back to his cage. "Is something the matter?"

Albert crammed a handful of marshmallows into his mouth and sighed. "I have a tummy ache, and a headache, too."

"Maybe you'd feel better if you exercised," Violet suggested.

"And maybe that would make me feel worse," Albert grumbled.

"You can't break training now! Boris is telling everyone he's going to beat you!"

"I'm too sick to race!" Albert said. "Go away and leave me alone."

Violet looked for Keeper Norman. She hoped he would know what to do.

“I’m sorry to hear you’re not feeling well,” Keeper Norman said when he came to visit Albert. “I think the zoo doctor should have a look at you right away.”

But after a thorough examination, the doctor could find nothing wrong.

“You’re in great shape to race on Saturday, Albert!” the doctor said. “In fact, I’m bringing my entire family to watch you run.”

At this news, Albert broke into a sweat and bolted for the door. Norman ran after him.

Albert stopped for a moment to catch his breath. “If my body’s well, why do I feel so awful?” he thought to himself.

Just then Keeper Norman caught up “I think I know what’s wrong,” he panted. “This race is giving you the jitters.”

He took out a pad of paper and began to write. “Here’s something that will help you to calm down so you can think clearly and do your best. I call it the Relaxercise.”

Albert’s ears perked up.

“You can remember the steps by spelling the word ‘relax,’” Keeper Norman said.

“R-E-L-A-X,” Albert spelled to himself as he read over Norman’s shoulder. “I hope it works!”

Albert grabbed the paper and ran back to his cage.

NORMAN'S R-E-L-A-XERCISE

Recognize that you're upset. Talk it over with someone you trust.

Ease your mind. Tell yourself you can calm down.

Loosen up. Take ten slow deep breaths.

Allow your imagination to help. Close your eyes and picture a place where you feel relaxed and happy.

X marks the end. Open your eyes when you feel calm.

"Will you coach me, Violet?" Albert asked after showing her the paper.

"Of course," Violet replied. She read the rule for 'R' aloud. "Recognize that you're upset. Talk it over with someone you trust."

Albert twiddled his fur. Finally he blurted out, "I'm afraid I'm going to lose the race to that big bully Boris and none of my friends will like me anymore!"

"Albert! Friendship has nothing to do with winning races," Violet said. "We'll like you no matter what!"

Albert gave a great sigh of relief.

Violet coached Albert through E, L, A, and X.

"How do you feel now?" she asked when they had finished.

Albert opened his eyes. "It worked! I calmed myself down!" He crumpled Norman's paper and tossed it into the trash. "Nothing will ever make me feel nervous again," he said. He grabbed his stopwatch and headed for the track.

Violet thought for a moment. Then she took the paper out of the trash and tucked it into her pocket.

Albert was glad to be back in training. He zoomed around the track, determined to break his best record.

"Melting snowballs!" Boris exclaimed, grabbing his binoculars. "It's Albert, and he's faster than ever! I've got to find a way to slow him down or I'm going to look like the biggest loser this side of the Rocky Mountains."

As Boris paced back and forth across his cage, he tripped over a hole. He looked down and saw a little gopher burrowing her way to safety.

"That's it!" he cried. "Gopher holes!"

Boris caught the little gopher by the tail. "If you help me win a very important race, I'll let you keep your tail!"

The gopher nodded her head. She was too frightened to speak.

"All you have to do is dig up the inside lane of the track," whispered Boris. "It'll be our little secret."

Boris let go of the gopher and watched her scurry off toward the track.

By sunset on Saturday, the bleachers were packed. When Albert arrived, Boris was waiting for him at the starting line.

"I've saved the inside lane for you, old sport," said Boris, throwing his arms just a little too tightly around Albert.

"We're supposed to flip a coin for the best lane," Albert protested.

"You have it," insisted Boris. "I won't need it."

As Albert took his position on the inside lane, he felt a familiar twinge of fear in the pit of his stomach.

Keeper Norman yelled, "On your mark, get set..."
"Good luck!" Boris barked.
Albert jumped the gun.
Norman started again. "On your mark, get set, go!"
"So long, slowpoke," Boris snickered. He took off like a shot, leaving Albert frozen in position at the starting line.

"Time out!" signaled Norman. "Albert needs a minute to calm down."
"That's no fair!" shouted Boris.
As Albert walked to the sidelines, he wished Boris had never come to the zoo.

Boris paraded around the track, flexing his muscles for the crowd.

"I'll never beat Boris," said Albert. "Just look at that show-off!"

"No, look at this," urged Violet, waving Norman's paper in front of his face.

"Now he's leading the crowd in a cheer for himself!" Albert moaned.

"B-O-R-I-S!" chanted the crowd.

"R-E-L-A-X!" coached Violet.

Albert put his head in his paws.

"You can do it!" Violet said. "Just concentrate!"

At last Albert heard Violet's words. He took the Relaxercise from her paw and did all the steps, from R to X. When Keeper Norman blew his whistle, Albert's eyes were still closed.

Violet leaned over and whispered, "Time-out is over. Where are you now?"

Albert whispered back, "Pretending I'm in my bed. I can smell the scent of marshmallows on my pillow and feel my teddy's tickly fur. And do you know what?"

"What?" asked Violet.

Albert's eyes flew open. "I'm ready to run!"

Keeper Norman made an announcement as Albert ran back to the starting line. "To be fair, for delaying the race, Albert must give up the inside lane to Boris."

A look of horror crossed Boris's face, but there was nothing he could do without revealing his plot. The two bears switched lanes.

"On your mark, get set, go!" Norman said.

The race had finally begun.

"I am Albert, the Running Bear, light as a feather, loose as a goose, and faster than a shooting star," chanted Albert as he sped around the track.

Suddenly howls of laughter from the crowd shattered his concentration.

"What's so funny?" he wondered.

Then Albert did something he had never done in a race before. He looked back. To his amazement, he saw Boris bouncing and zigzagging down the inside lane.

"Here's my chance," Boris panted as Albert turned to stare. Forgetting the gopher holes, Boris took a great leap forward. He landed neck and neck with Albert, and the two bears charged on. Each was intent upon breaking the tape, which was only a few yards away.

Albert edged ahead, running as hard as he could. He did not notice Boris freeze in mid-stride, his foot caught in the last gopher hole. Nor did he see Boris fall with a thud, toppled like a giant spruce tree.

Albert lunged across the finish line. Keeper Norman declared him the winner, but this time there was little applause. A hush came over the crowd as they watched Boris struggle to free his foot.

"What happened?" cried Albert as he ran to Boris's side. At that moment, the little gopher popped her head out of a hole.

"I'm s-sorry you tripped," she stuttered. "But you did tell me to dig up the inside lane!"

"So that's why you wanted me to have the inside lane!" Albert exploded. "Those gopher holes were meant for me!"

"Where I come from, it's every bear for himself," said Boris.

"Here at the zoo," said Albert, "being a good sport is more important than winning a race."

"That's easy for you to say. You never lose!" Boris grumbled.

"But you might have won fair and square!" said Albert.

Boris looked away, but not quickly enough to hide the quiver in his lower lip. Suddenly he did not look so enormous.

Albert's anger began to fade.

"Come on," Albert said, helping Boris to his feet. "We'd better have the zoo doctor look at your ankle. You'll need to be in good shape for our rematch."

"Rematch?" Boris repeated in amazement. "You'd give me another chance?"

"Sure," said Albert. "You're the biggest challenge I've ever had."

A smile brightened Boris's face as he hobbled off the track, leaning on Albert for support. And the crowd applauded them both.

That night, as Albert crawled into bed, a paper airplane sailed into his cage and landed on his pillow. There was a message written on the wing. It said:

Two, four, six, eight.
I think Albert's
really great.

Yours truly,
Boris

A Note to the Reader

Just like Albert, the Running Bear, all of us get the "jitters" sometimes. This usually happens when we are feeling under a lot of pressure or stress. Some stress is necessary. Without it, we would feel bored and unchallenged. But too much stress can make us feel cranky, frightened, and even sick. Here are some situations that are likely to cause stress:

Taking a test
Competing in sports
Performing in front of others
Having a fight with a friend
Starting school
Parents fighting
Being teased
Feeling left out

What kinds of situations do you find stressful?

Often, when we experience stress, we feel panic or anger. Sometimes we blame our problem on someone, or something, else. In some cases, we even try to pretend that there's nothing wrong. Unfortunately, none of these reactions helps us feel better. In fact, our bodies may send us "signals" to let us know that we are still upset. Here are some common signals your body might send:

Upset stomach
Headaches
Sleeplessness
Sweaty palms
Pounding heart
Irritability
Nervous habits
Fear that something bad will happen
Forgetfulness

How does your body tell you when you are feeling stress?

The key to coping with stress is learning how to relax. When we are able to relax, we can think clearly and find a way to handle our problems. Then we can do our best. This sounds quite simple, but it is not always easy to relax when you are feeling nervous or upset. Here is how the Relaxercise can work for you.

Recognize that you're upset. Talk it over with someone you trust.
Once you're aware of your own body signals, you will be able to recognize when you are feeling stress. By talking over your problem with someone who knows and cares about you, the way Albert talked to Violet, you will feel a great relief in just getting things off your chest.

Ease your mind. Tell yourself that you can calm down.
Knowing that you do have the power to calm yourself down, you will feel less helpless and more in control. This knowledge helped Albert to get back on the track and run his best race against Boris.

Loosen up. Take ten slow, deep breaths.
Whenever you feel nervous, frightened, or upset, there are changes in the way you breathe. You begin to take rapid, shallow breaths like Albert did after Boris's challenge. In order to relax, remember to breathe slowly and deeply, using the lower part of your lungs. Push hard on the "out" breath rather than on the "in" breath. By breathing this way, you will begin to loosen up those tense muscles. Continue slow, deep breathing until the end of the Relaxercise.

Allow your imagination to help. Close your eyes and picture a place where you feel relaxed and happy.
Train your mind to take you away to your special place. No matter where you are, this will help you calm down even when you are under a lot of pressure. Albert liked to imagine his cozy bed with his special pillow and his teddy bear. What favorite place would you choose to imagine?

X marks the end. Open your eyes when you feel calm.
We can't promise that your problem will magically disappear at the end of the Relaxercise. But we do hope that you will feel more relaxed and able to cope with stress. Good luck in whatever challenges come your way!

Sincerely,
the Authors